NOKMA &
THE
UNFAIRY
TALES

RAJNEESH JASWAL

Dedicated to my maternal grandmother (Aamma), who passed to heavenly abode in 2007.

Contents

Preface   *vii*

1. Nokma & His Camera   1

2. The Gutsy Feast   8

3. Costly Affair   11

4. The Counselling   15

5. Inception   18

6. Negatives Of The Roll   23

7. Floods; Blessing In Disguise   27

8. Flood & Fury   33

9. Farewell   36

10. The Troubled Waters   41

11. Farm Fiasco   48

12. Sail To Strife   54

13. The Resurrection   60

14. In Alien Land   65

15. The Follow Up   70

16. Too Close But Too Far   73

Preface

"Nokma & the Unfairy tales", is a merger of fiction and reality. Author was one of the twenty odd students who were exchanged with a batch of same number, amongst two Navodaya Vidyalayas, as part of their migration policy to promote the national integration. The two states in this case were randomly picked as Himachal Pradesh and Meghalaya. The prodigies from different schools were thrown in a shared dormitory to yield symphony out of cacophony. There were stories told, retold, lived, and sometimes even relived. A teenager who himself lived and relived these stories for years, decides to write them all, weaving them into a single plot.

Nokma, the central character is a typical native Garo man, faced with some stiff challenges in order to earn a livelihood, right since his school days. He tries job after job, but only to fail. However, each of his endeavor rewards him with the requisite experience inevitable for his next sojourn. He does dodge the destiny many a time in the process, but only to discover that it was the destiny which eventually dodged him.

The journey eventually lands him at his favorite destination and he wins accolades for what he does best, but the reward once again is in terms of losing something very dear. It is a story of redemption of contentment shrouded in failures.

Besides the storyline, it's an attempt to understand the typical North Eastern culture, the tribal livelihoods, the social usages in the light of matriarchy and matrilineal set up. The problems of tribal people in border areas, the cross border scuffles, the demographic disorders and the insurgency in North East, and the consequent shift in the mental psyche of the inhabitants.

ONE

NOKMA & HIS CAMERA

"*Nokma* needn't even remind his subjects to wear that customary smile before he would click a photograph. He would always wear a perpetual funny smile on his chubby face, especially while holding his *Yashika* camera; the sitters would automatically follow and would smile back into his camera.

Nokma used to be surrounded by lot of young people, especially girls. One would often find him busy explaining; 'the photograph was absolutely fine and that the one she was holding was better off, than all the previous ones'. Thirty five rupees, was the amount he would charge for three copies, and not to mention, it was mandatory to buy all the three.

"*Nokma*! This is not done. I am to send this photograph to *Dipika*. Look at my face! It's sulking." I raised protest finding *Nokma* relatively free the other day.

"Hey, who is *Dipika*? You never told me you were getting those clicked for her." *Nokma* asked raising his eyebrows.

"*Dipika Hazong*, my pen friend from *Williamnagar*. She asked for my photograph in her last letter." I disclosed shyly.

"Oh! I see. *Hazong* girls are extremely beautiful. She needs to be sent the finest photograph. Girls are blessed with typical aesthetic sense. A casual one could well ruin your chances. I am afraid these photographs need to be clicked again." *Nokma* announced while shuffling all the three copies in his hands.

"*Nokma!* Does it mean I will be charged thirty five rupees again?" I asked while lodging my protest at the same time.

"I am afraid you will be. Love has a cost dear, and especially when it's a beautiful girl. We will have to shoot outdoors; 'indoor photography' won't do in this case. I have few locations in my mind. We can give it a shot as soon as we are blessed with a sunny day." *Nokma* threw an offer respecting my right to acceptance.

Thankfully, we were blessed with a sunny day the very next morning. I ironed my *tericot* shirt, cherry blossomed my shoes, shaved my yet to be grown whiskers, applied *boroline* on my face, conditioned my hair using coconut oil and readied myself to venture into some unknown locations in South Garo Hills of Meghalaya, in the north eastern part of India.

I was in class 10, while *Nokma* was in Class 12. Both of us were supposed to bunk a couple of classes, though it wasn't quite advisable as we were to appear in CBSE Board exams at the end of the session. Still, both of us settled for it because of our own motivations.

Nokma's camera was minting money for him. *Navodaya* School *Baghmara* had strength of some six hundred odd. Out of those, some four hundred were potential customers of *Nokma*. Besides, he had settled it with principal, that any group photo, passport size photo, or any other photo would be clicked and sold by him only.

We kept on walking along the river *Rompha* on a broken down country road near *Baghmara, South Garo Hills*, undoubtedly one of the best parts of the world. The relatively smaller hills are adorned with evergreen subtropical forests. The wettest place of the world is home to some rarest species of flora and fauna.

As soon as we started walking our way into the picturesque valley, I realized this outing was far more interesting than what my classes used to be.

Like any other Garo man, *Nokma* was a very powerfully built man. His pants would generally be folded up to his knees exposing his very strong calves. His entire body was naturally crafted to give him V-shape. His hair were often too dry, his eyes partly red swollen and skin tanned. His height could have been a few inches more but still he was a smart man and would make a statement while walking.

"*Nokma*! Why are you called *Nokma*?" I asked with no sense of purpose.

"*Nokma* is a village headman in *Garo Hills*."

"So, you are a village headman?"

"No, my father was, and friends started calling me *Nokma*."

"Oh! What does your father do now?"

"He is no more."

"Oh! I am sorry. What happened?"

"He was shot at near border."

"Shot? But why?"

"He tried to sneak into Bangladesh."

"Bangladesh? But why did he try to do that?"

"He was into a business. He would bring cheap clothes from Bangladesh and sell those here with higher prices. Likewise some of the items he would take from here, and sell those in Bangladesh. Unfortunately his timings and modus operandi coincided with those of some notorious smugglers who were into the business of narcotics, and that got him shot. But he wasn't into the narcotics." The smile disappeared for a while from *Nokma's* face while he revealed something very secret from in his mind.

"I am sorry but who are those notorious smugglers into the business of narcotics, and what's their modus operandi?" I asked with a clear sense of purpose this occasion.

"Indo-Bangla border is not as stringent as Indo-Pak border. Hundreds of people cross border in the morning and return in the evening to earn livelihood. They are extremely poor people and BSF men allow them after checking and frisking. But the persons with ulterior intentions have to take the river route. They dive into the river *Simsang* this side and would get out of it the other side across the border, escaping the eye of both BSF and BDR (Bangladesh Rifles) men. The other day BSF had a tip-off that some of the members from the notorious gang are crossing the river stealthily and they fired some blind shots into the waters. My father was shot while he was under water in the river as his timing of crossing coincided with that of the notorious gang. His body was recovered on the other side of the border and even the dead body couldn't be brought back, as that would have put us all in trouble. We just lodged the missing complaint with the police and never claimed the body. We didn't get any compensation as the rules are such that police can issue a death certificate only after seven years since a person has gone missing." *Nokma* simplified everything for me but I could notice a teardrop rolling down his cheek.

"I am sorry *Nokma*, let's talk something else." These words of mine put the smile back on his face.

"Do you know where we are going?" *Nokma* was quick to ask.

"We are going for a photo-shoot, *Nokma*." I replied promptly.

"You are right, but you are also going to visit my house." *Nokma* surprised me with this revelation.

"Oh really? That's exciting." I definitely wanted to see a Garo House from close, meet people, to have an insight into their culture and so on.

We were a group of twenty odd students who were migrated from one of the similar schools of Himachal Pradesh for two years, class 9 and 10. Right since their inception, Navodaya Schools or *Navodaya Vidyalayas* had this unique convention of exchanging students amongst two different states, with an objective of promoting national integration. Though it had its problems as well but by and large we had adapted to it.

Normally we were advised to not to venture outside, as we were readily conspicuous for our different features. This was also because of the reason that tribal people were extremely suspicious of outsiders. However, with *Nokma* around, I was relieved a great degree.

It was a beautiful house, all woven with bamboo splits, which were plastered with laterite to add meat to the walls. The house was roofed so beautifully with dry grass and leaves that it resembled a painting on the wall. It had a boundary wall and gate, all made up of bamboo splits. There were flower beds all around the house along with the boundary wall, where the flowers of myriad hues were blossoming. Some hens were feeding from a small courtyard, which felt disturbed as we entered the gate.

There was a small gazebo all made of bamboo, a table and a couple of chairs around it, where I was made to sit.

Nokma made me to stand in the garden holding a flower, before shouting the cliché, 'smile please', and a flash completed the purpose for which we had actually travelled this far, bunking our classes.

"This is for *Dipika Hazong*, and now you can sit back on the chair." *Nokma* smiled as usual looking at his camera before leaving.

As soon as I occupied my seat, *Nokma's* mother came with tea and *Tambul* (betel leaf) for pan chewing. I wished her with phrases tailored in local dialect, the Garo, which I had managed to learn in the company of *Nokma*. She kept on talking to me for minutes. She could neither speak Hindi nor English, I could barely speak Garo, but her gestures were so telling that I understood everything she said, and also that she wanted me to have lunch with them.

After about an hour *Nokma* appeared with two bowls, and a rice plate. While putting down one bowl, he told me that one of the hens was roasted for lunch, whereas the other bowl had *Nakham*, the dry fish curry.

His mom kept watching straight into my face as I ate from the plate. She made me to recognize the hen I was eating, the one that came very close to me while I entered the gate.

"We are only two. She works very hard in the fields to grow rice. I try to earn some money from photography. Let's see how long it goes. I will have to change my profession if it stops paying dividends." *Nokma* said smilingly while putting a leg piece in my plate.

I had to answer so many questions from *Nokma's* mom while eating. She was very much interested in the topography and climate of my state. She also asked about our marriage rituals and inheritance rights. I also had to explain rituals practiced during birth and last rites. She simultaneously compared those with the ones prevalent amongst Garo people and apprised me about them.

We finished the sumptuous food and departed after putting *Tambul* leaves in our mouths.

As soon as we reached campus, *Nokma* promised that I will get three copies after a week.

"You will surely get her photograph in return", *Nokma* assured me with his trademark smile.

Seven days were a little too long to wait and my patience relented only in couple of days. I decided to write to *Dipika* sans photograph, while at the same time asking her to send her photograph first, as mine was still under process.

Someone told me that it could actually take even longer. Thirty six photographs have to be clicked before *Nokma* would take out the negative camera roll and send it to the dark room for final prints. This prompted me to put the letter in red letter box of our school the very same evening I wrote it.

TWO
THE GUTSY FEAST

Nokma was extremely hard working but still somehow his studies were suffering. Students of both the board classes were shifted to a single dormitory having double decker beds, so I had a clear chance to watch *Nokma's* activities. He would escape to his house every alternate day, which wasn't permissible in a boarding school like that of ours.

When in hostel, *Nokma* would be busy all the time with his camera. And when he was not with his camera, he would be busy sharpening his knives and daggers. He was a great hunter as well. For that matter the entire *Garo* people were great hunters and that's how the place got its name, *Baghmara*. One of the brave men had killed a tiger to name the town.

One fine afternoon, *Nokma* came very tired from somewhere. He was feeling hungry but was already too late for lunch in the school mess. He called me along with two other *Himachali* boys for some help. A herd of goat was grazing in the lawn just outside the hostel. He looked calmly at his prey, looked all sides, and once he found it opportune, he abducted a goat into the hostel.

"We have only two hours. We will have to eat it after doing all the procedures within the stipulated time." *Nokma's* orders were very clear.

He took his long and sharp knives and daggers out, and started the operation. We were assisting in awe as live dissection was first experience for all of us. Within minutes *Nokma* tore apart the skin and segregated the eatables parts from the non-eatables ones.

"You! Open the chamber of septic tank and abandon it all there." *Nokma* packed the wastage in a sack and ordered thus to one of the fellows.

There was a small store room in the backyard of hostel dormitories which housed the old furniture. *Nokma* opened its window and got into it with his entire team. He took two wooden chairs and rammed them against one another to get many small wooden pieces. He put those in a small tin canister and lit the fire. The pieces of meat were pierced into the sharp bamboo splits and spokes of small bicycle wheels. All of us were soon asked to barbeque the stuff. *Nokma* kept on instructing how far to keep it from the flame, when to rotate and when to stop. The exercise lasted for nearly 45 minutes till *Nokma* called off the operation after tasting a piece from the spoke I was holding. He had some salt packed in his pocket and he instructed us to use it as per the taste requirements.

We all were eating something which was so tasty yet frightening. The owner of the herd would normally come in the evening to collect his goats. He would walk with a long bamboo stick and a sharp dagger tied at its one end. The idea of his catching us red handed was acting as a deterrent to the taste. We still managed to eat briskly. All of us must have eaten three to four kilo grams of meat in total. *Nokma* made us to clean every single bone, the blood stains, and every single hair even, before the fire was properly extinguished and all its remains were thrown in the river *Rompha*. The room was restored to its original before being closed.

The owner of herd walked into the hostel in evening, enquiring about his missing goat. *Nokma* who had just come out of the toilet, politely refused to have an idea about.

"Goat rearing is no longer profitable now. For last one month I have lost five of my goats to wild predators." The owner lamented before *Nokma*.

"Same in my case *Musa*, it's a full time job now. Can't really leave it to chance", *Nokma* cautioned wisely and the owner left dejected.

THREE

COSTLY AFFAIR

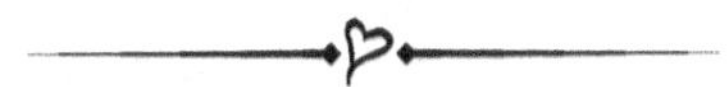

Next morning we all skipped the morning drills in ground as those weren't mandatory for board classes. However, the real reason was that we had had a very heavy dinner the last night. We woke up late and that too because of some distant noises. Out of curiosity we rushed to the scene along with *Nokma*.

It was somewhere near teacher's quarters, not very far from our mess or dining hall. A man was tied with jute ropes around a tree and was being whipped with a leather string. The man looked familiar and as we approached nearer, we figured him out. He was our school clerk who hailed from Delhi. *Nokma* slowly neared the scene and came back with an update, after enquiring from an elderly lady.

"What happened *Nokma*?" I asked straightway.

"He was caught red handed with a lady." *Nokma* whispered in my ears.

"What do you mean red handed?" I couldn't make it for a while.

"The lady used to supply milk to the man every morning and ended up being in relationship with him. Her husband followed her this morning and found them in compromising position. He is paying for that now. This is *Nokma's* justice." *Nokma* clarified though I still was not clear what did the phrase red handed mean in that case.

"What do you mean? Did you pronounce this judgment?" I asked even more inquisitively.

"No, the real *Nokma* of the village did that." *Nokma* reminded me with that, that he wasn't the real one.

"But wasn't the lady guilty as well, *Nokma*?"

"Oh certainly she is. But she will not be thrashed publically and of course to this degree. Ours is a matrilineal, matriarchal society and women enjoy precedence over men in all matters. She will be given a chance to admit her sin and beg forgiveness. She can also choose to part her ways from her husband." *Nokma* clarified.

"Oh I see. But *Nokma* what if she admits her mistake but still wants to stay with her husband, and her husband on the contrary doesn't want to live with her?" I asked with little sense of justice I had till then.

"She will get benefit of doubt on at least one occasion, maybe she fell prey to some notorious design by the man. Her husband will have to accept her in that case, but not if she turns out to be a habitual offender." *Nokma* clarified further.

Our School teachers and staff members were also trying to mediate but in vain. Our Principal reached the scene just then and rushed to area which was supposedly out of bounds for him. He received a powerful flying kick and tumbled down the small hill. His glasses were broken and he didn't move for about two minutes after landing.

As everyone rushed to help the aged man, *Nokma* sensing the emergency or to score over others, thought it wise to inform Principal's family and therefore rushed immediately to Principal's residence.

"*Principal Sir ko vo log mar diya*", *Nokma* tried to speak Hindi to ma'am who was from Bihar.

Ma'am fainted there and then; her daughter who was also a student of our school started crying. *Nokma* had no idea that he actually communicated it to their belief that Principal was actually killed.

He waited but situation worsened; Mrs. Principal lost her consciousness and fell down. *Nokma* immediately rushed to the 'school sister' for help narrating the incident.

Madam Sister was from Manipur who arrived soon taking all the troubles walking past in her shawl which was actually wrapped around her waist very much like Sari. As soon as she reached she sprinkled some water on Ma'am Principal's face. Ma'am opened her eyes to discover that Principal was being helped by two teachers to walk into the house. *Nokma's* information kept them baffled for some time till it was cleared by principal sir himself that it must have been because of language problem. *Nokma* apologized but realized that this effort of him was not taken in a good taste.

Back at the conflict zone School clerk was spared with a stern warning and all our school staff was threatened to face dire consequences if they didn't behave well.

Tribal people are mostly intrinsic communities, highly suspicious of outsiders. There were many instances of skirmishes which took ugly turns with outsiders at receiving end. Our school clerk had really played with fire this occasion and the consequences were for everyone from outside.

The very next day *Nokma* got the message that the verbal contract given to him for clicking the photographs of 600 odd students for Identity cards has been terminated and was given to someone else from the market. He was supposed to get five rupees a copy and the loss grossed to 3000/- rupees.

FOUR

THE
COUNSELLING

Mishra sir, our English teacher would routinely follow his visits to hostel dormitories and counsel his students on all problems they confronted, ranging from studies to their day to day life. He was an exceptional counselor who would readily make out that someone was in need of it. His experience of working in various fields, ranging from his services as announcer in All India Radio to an English teacher gave him an edge over rest of his counterparts, in gauging and sorting out the dilemmas faced by the students.

One fine evening when Mishra Sir was on a routine visit to hostel, he could easily make out that something was disturbing *Nokma*, and that he was on his study table with his book open but with his mind somewhere else.

"What happened dear, Is everything all right?" Mishra Sir asked with utmost humility.

"Good evening sir, yes I am all right, trying to concentrate on my studies." *Nokma* almost dodged the question.

"That's nice to hear from you. Feel free to tell me if you are not able to." Mishra sir knew how to pull a rabbit out of hat.

"Sir, I am trying to focus hard but the fear of failing in board exams still looms large, I don't know why." *Nokma* spilled the beans after a silence for couple of minutes as Mishra sir continued to look straight into his eyes with empathy.

"Well first of all we got to find if it's really the fear of exams, or is it something else which preoccupies your mind? Is everything fine back home? Are you sure you aren't bothered by anything else?" Mishra sir pressed the jugular vein.

"You are right sir; actually I lost some three thousand odd rupees. Principal Sir and his family misunderstood me completely. I never meant that." This confession of *Nokma* came with teary eyes and Mishra sir pressed his hand as if he wanted him to speak more.

"My mother needs consistent financial support. The paddy crop was washed away in floods this season. She works very hard to make us self-sufficient, but money is still needed for our daily expenses." *Nokma* felt relieved while he disclosed it to Mishra sir.

"Oh! I see. Can't you manage till your exams?" Mishra sir asked.

"I have enough money for now but it will be very difficult once the exams are over. We will be requiring money for the poultry feed and for the next season's seed." *Nokma* revealed his fears.

Mishra sir took a white sheet and drew a glass on it, half filled with water and half empty.

"Have a look at this glass, it has two connotations.

One, that it is half filled.

Two, that it is half empty.

Now both are equally true. But at this stage if we look at the empty part only, we may not be able to use the filled part to our advantage. Conversely, if we make best of what we have, we have a fair chance of getting the empty part replenished." *Nokma* was listening to it very carefully.

"You will easily get into the two years Junior Basic Teacher Training Program at North Eastern Teacher's Training institute here in this very town, so near to your home. And I tell you what, this is absolutely free as government offers 100% subsidy on these seats to promote education in tribal areas. All you have to do is just pass your twelfth class exam with minimum of 50% marks." Mishra sir noted a spark in *Nokma's* eyes as he made this revelation.

"Oh! Really sir? I wasn't aware about this. It sounds great."

"Not only that, you are guaranteed a government job just after you finish this course. Last year they could only fill 50% of the total seats, so there is a backlog besides this year's seats. Government has opened huge number of primary schools but they are running sans teachers. So you are very likely to be posted in one of the nearest schools around your home, unlike me who has come all the way from Allahabad." Mishra sir smiled and put that trademark smile of *Nokma* back on his face.

"Thank you so much sir. I will surely do it the way you told me to." Nokma smiled in his original.

Mishra sir left with that note and *Nokma* was back into studies.

FIVE

INCEPTION

I was desperately waiting for my photographs. I enquired from *Nokma* on couple of occasions but the camera roll of 36 photographs was yet to be filled with images of its destined subjects. *Nokma* had many rounds of girl's hostel but girls were already into studies and shying away from anything like that.

One fine evening the girls were filling their water bottles from a natural spring, slightly uphill, at a walking distance from our school's mess. *Nokma* was carrying his camera with him besides his water bottle and was simultaneously looking for customers.

A girl who had just joined our school sprinkled some water on her face after filling her water bottle. *Nokma* actually saw her for the first time and couldn't just resist the infatuations. He spontaneously flashed at least twice before she came to know about it.

"How dare you to click my photographs without my permission." The girl lodged a vociferous protest once she knew that she was being photographed.

"I am sorry, but don't worry, you will get the copies and I am sure you won't regret it. These are your signature photographs which you can keep as memoirs. I am a professional photographer, you can confirm. You posed so nicely that I couldn't resist. Had I asked you, it would have destroyed the natural pose." *Nokma* tried to clarify.

"I am asking, how dare you to click my photograph without my permission?" the girl didn't seem convinced by *Nokma's* pleas.

"I am sorry ma'am, but you are unnecessarily making an issue out of it. I will hand over the pictures to you only." *Nokma* made another attempt.

The girl started crying and it infuriated *Nokma*. He took out the camera roll and banged it against the concrete wall. It shattered into pieces, and so did many hopes with all the photographs, including those of mine.

Naobi, the only girl in the contingent of five, was migrated from *Vishnupur*, a school of our kind in Manipur. They were migrated in mid-session because of the fact that the *Naga-Kuki* struggle had ensued after a long ceasefire. The board classes were shifted to the neighboring states and other classes were sent back home in the wake of disturbances.

Naobi was *Meitei*, an ethnic tribe of Manipur. Both *Nokma* and *Naobi* were in the same class but she never saw *Nokma* in the class. This could also have been the reason that she resented the act of *Nokma*. But she didn't like *Nokma* destroying the entire camera roll as well. Everyone was dejected over this anticlimax at the natural spring site that evening.

Naobi was very upset with what happened. She was extremely emotional and couldn't have her dinner that night. She became more upset when she came to know about *Nokma's* financial condition, and that his father was no more, and that he was into photography only to support his family.

Both *Nokma* and *Naobi* missed classes for two consecutive days as they didn't dare facing each other. It was more difficult for *Naobi*, as she thought she overreacted and that she was guilty. She decided to break the shackles and called upon *Nokma* via special messenger. *Nokma* turned up but was very apprehensive as it was yet to be settled.

"Why didn't you ask me if you wanted my photographs? I would never have said no." *Naobi* tried to be humble.

"The photographs were for you only. I would have returned them to you. I do it to earn some money. I have photographed the entire school. It was a good pose and I thought you might like it." *Nokma* uttered in one go and it looked like a readymade script he had learnt by heart.

"I am sorry, you entire camera roll got destroyed because of this. But now I want some photographs of mine here, amidst the beautiful Garo Hills." *Naobi* said while trying to control her smile.

"You can always have ma'am, but I am not left with camera rolls now." *Nokma* made a plain confession.

"Here is one brand new for you." *Naobi* had come all prepared and put forth a brand new camera roll.

"No I can't take this roll." *Nokma* expressed his inability.

"I will start crying", threatened *Naobi*. *Naobi* had really come all prepared. She knew that this ploy of crying would never miss the target especially if aimed at boys.

"Okay, let me take it." *Nokma* fell shortly to prove the gospel.

"Take me for a walk on Sunday. I will have a feel of beautiful Garo hills and some photographs."

Both of them smiled to convey something before leaving.

Nokma was feeling great but he lost his connection with his studies again. Waiting till Sunday turned difficult. The aftereffect of half-filled glass theory of Mishra Sir subsided altogether. *Nokma* quickly fitted the roll in his camera and kept waiting till Sunday.

Naobi was looking absolutely gorgeous in her red gown on the appointed day. Her fringe hairstyle allowed some hair to fall on her forehead, *Sadhna cut*, as it matched the hair style of *Sadhana*, the Bollywood Diva. Her eyes were sparkling and could perhaps reciprocate to any gesture the way she wanted. Though styled to optimum, she chose to wear modesty and would walk graciously.

She persuaded two junior girls to escort her. On the very same lines, *Nokma* persuaded me to escort, so that it looked like a group and people couldn't read much between the lines.

Everything followed the very same way it had followed the other day. *Nokma* chose the very same location, the very same destination for the photo-shoot. The other two girls were Garo girls, so obviously the Manipuri girl caught the eye of *Nokma's* mother. They spoke tirelessly without understanding even a single word from the languages of one another.

Everything was followed by lunch, for which yet another hen was killed from the poultry. In the meanwhile *Nokma* exhausted the entire camera roll with just two snaps of mine. All others included the two girls, his mother, with *Naobi* featuring in most of them. We had a great day and came back singing and enjoying.

Back in the hostel, I found a letter for me.

"It looks as if you just want my photograph and don't want to give your own. This I found is a breach of trust. Don't write to me again. I won't be responding anymore."

It was a clarion call from *Dipika Hazong* and chances of it culminating into a story had more than vanished. Those were the days of making pen friends and my first blind attempt was dispatched to disdain.

SIX

NEGATIVES OF THE ROLL

The negatives of the roll were immediately sent to the dark room and prints were received in no time. *Nokma* relaxed the rule of mandatory three copies this occasion, but made sure to obtain atleast two copies of all photographs which featured *Naobi*, one for *Naobi* and other for himself. He rather bought an album and placed all her photographs diligently in.

Nokma approached me the same evening and advanced two different copies featuring me.

"Look how smart you look in these photographs. *Dipika* must be very happy once she receives these pictures of you." *Nokma* uttered smiling naughtily.

"It's all over now; she has already made it clear that she won't be responding to any of my letters now. Let me just keep them as souvenirs." I responded with minimal excitement.

Nokma felt sorry for me as his silence suggested, but he had actually come for different reason. He wanted me to write something for *Naobi. Nokma* wanted to gift her with an album of her photographs, with some thoughts inscribed on it.

"What exactly do you want me write on it *Nokma*?"

I wasn't sure about the feelings of *Nokma*.

"That's why I came to you because I don't have any idea."

Even *Nokma* wasn't sure about his feelings.

"But still let me know what you want to convey." I again tried to press.

"I just want to thank her and wish her with friendly quotes. You know I can't do it with words." *Nokma* must have curtailed his thoughts as his gestures would suggest.

"Are you sure you just want to be friendly only, I can already sense there is something more to it." I tried to put words in his mouth.

"No nothing of that sort, but yes I like her. I don't want to disturb her as the exams are approaching and it could be detrimental to both of us if we engage in something more. Let the time ripe and I will cut the ice." *Nokma* summed up diplomatically.

I followed in latter and spirit and used best of words I knew, to thank her as desired by *Nokma*.

"Let me take this opportunity to thank you from the bottom of my heart, for you helped me out from the guilt of taking your photographs without your permission. Not only that you made up for my destroyed camera roll, but happily walked to see my mother. She was very happy to see you as well. I am enclosing all your photographs in a small album which I am sure you will cherish for rest of your life. Wish you all the best for your studies." The draft was approved by *Nokma* which he chose to write on his own, with prefixes and suffixes.

Meanwhile I put all my photographs in my note book but assured myself that someday I will also buy an album for them.

"Why don't you just send one of the photographs to *Dipika*. Who knows she might reply enclosing one of her own." *Nokma* tried to instill some hope as he saw me putting those photographs in my note book.

"No, I am afraid that will amount to breach of trust again. Let it be the way it is now." I replied with a sense of denial.

Nokma called the special messenger and immediately sent the packet to girl's hostel. Just after ten minutes news came in that she received the packet happily.

Nokma couldn't hide the happiness and kept on watching those photographs endlessly. However, he was anxious as he was expecting a reply. Two days lapsed but he didn't get anything in writing. They crossed a couple of times during lunch break or dinner time, the smiles exchanged, but *Nokma* didn't get anything in black and white. He was deeply engulfed into the pictures of *Naobi*, and would keep watching them tirelessly. I didn't know whether he was in love with *Naobi* or not, but he sure was in love with her pictures.

This had something serious to do with his studies. He would sit on his study table for long hours with his books wide open, but with his mind somewhere else. He himself had an idea that he was not studying. Classes used to be a very strict in school, offering no time for students to engage in conversations. Lunch break after classes was an opportunity, but girls would generally occupy a single table and *Naobi* would hardly break out from the shell.

The only opportunity left was during the games period, but there was dichotomy in the choices of the games they played. *Nokma* was good at playing carom only and that confined him to indoors. Whereas *Naobi* was a very good athlete and would at times play Volleyball, Badminton and even Football. *Nokma* did try his hand in Volleyball for that matter, but he would either bang the ball in nets or would hit it outside the court. He had to retreat soon from the game as he was becoming a laughing stock.

The chain of events resulted into loss of communication and the consequent withering away of feelings, which were yet to confluence. Engagement and dialogue are the most important factors for love stories to mushroom. Absence of any of these can rule out the possibility of friendships getting translated into romantic associations. There were widening gaps which needed to be plugged.

Nokma was in a fix. He could neither learn the game of volleyball, nor could he unlearn the idea of nearing *Naobi*.

SEVEN

FLOODS; BLESSING IN DISGUISE

Garo hills are the wettest place on earth as it's almost raining every time here in this part the world. There comes a time during the rainy season when rivers are flooded to worst. The school was located slightly in the outskirts of *Baghmara* which actually was a Doab between the rivers *Rompha* and *Simsang*. Both the rivers would flood to fill the gap and would join each other turning the campus of our school into a water pool. The existing school building was a makeshift arrangement built on the flood plain of river *Ropmha*. The site for the new buildings was finalized, but construction was yet to start. It was during flood days that we had to migrate slightly uphill. The design of the campus was such that both boy's hostel and girl's hostel were at the receiving ends. Class rooms were slightly elevated and therefore relatively safer. It was only our dining hall and the teacher's quarters, which were sufficiently uphill to avoid the river's fury.

Water level started rising suddenly one afternoon and hit the hostel floor around 3 PM. Principal along with warden immediately rushed to hostels.

"All the boarders who lodge on lower berths of double decker beds will fold their beddings in *holdall,* and will put them on upper berth of the bed. All the books and whatever belongings you have, put those on racks. Pack a small bag with your daily routine kit, one spare dress, towel and shoes, and immediately walk to assemble at classroom building". Principal Sahib instructed hurriedly and left to his own residence which was equally vulnerable for being at similar height.

On the other hand girl's hostel was evacuated on similar terms except for the fact that they were asked to take refuge in the dining hall. This was an irritant to many boys and girls who were looking to turn adversities into opportunities. As soon as boys assembled in their respective classrooms, water level started rising. Principal instructed everyone to head to student's mess or the dining hall immediately.

As everyone followed Principal Sahib, *Nokma* pulled me back along with three others and asked to wait. He took us to his classroom where he had just killed a wild boar who was struggling to escape the rampaging water.

"*Nokma,* but is it safe to stay back here? Water level is rising alarmingly." I enquired.

"We have wooden benches here; we can join them to make a platform. We can raise the height of the platform up to 8 feet approximately like that. My experience says in a worst case scenario the water level will elevate to 4 or 5 feet only." *Nokma* elaborated sounding experienced.

Just when the *Nokma* and his men were at work, Principal sir came back to have a final look if everyone had left.

"What the hell are you doing? No one will stay here. Just follow me to the dining room." Principal *Sahib* seemed disproportionately angry, but thankfully he didn't see the preparation for a non-veg feast underway, or else he could have thrashed us.

We all followed the orders in spirit and sat silently around a table in the dining hall once we reached. It was a tough situation for the school administration but students were literally enjoying. There were indoors games being played, songs erupting, and some were dancing to the tunes spontaneously. However, we the *Nokma* group, were feeling like odd one outs.

"I think we need to escape once we have our dinner. *Achhu* (grandpa, the term coined for principal) won't bother once we have our dinner." *Nokma* was still thinking about the wild boar.

"But it could be risky *Nokma*. Water level is on the rise and rain hasn't stopped even for a while." I tried to convince *Nokma* as I overheard some girls advocating my presence being on their side in the *Antakshari* competition. Suddenly, I didn't feel like leaving this place with such an electric atmosphere.

Rain was at its best; or perhaps at its worst. The tin roofing was making it absolutely difficult to hear anything loud and clear. To make anything audible, the lips speaking were automatically being drawn closer to the ear listening. There was no question of electricity as the electric pole just outside the dining hall was already uprooted. As the dark took over, some small candles were placed on tables, which were surrounded by wooden benches flanked by boys and girls in tandem.

There were at least two good singers who could play guitar as well. They set their orchestra in one of the corners and started performing hard rock, which eventually drew most of the boys to surround them and to dance to the tunes. As a result, some of the boys and most of the girls, who had taste for the Hindi romantic numbers of 90's, were left out. It was one such group where I found *Naobi* sitting. She was not very involved though and seemed confused. The two girls, who escorted us for the photo shoot to *Nokma's* house the other day, were sitting alongside.

"Hey come on join us, we are running out of songs", asked one of the girls sitting alongside *Naobi*, as I leaned closer to her face to make out what she was saying.

I fitted myself in the narrow space created by two girls who slipped apart on the wooden bench they were occupying. *Nokma* joined on the other side of the table and *Antakshari* began. Any song had to be discussed in the ears, and both my ears could hear from either side; the songs and the intent. Sometimes the whole cheek was being offered in the guise of ear, to be brought closer to the lips, in order to beat that deafening sound of rain on the rooftop. I being from Hindi belt, set the tone by singing some popular romantic numbers.

On the other side was the team of *Nokma* and *Naobi*. *Nokma* barely knew a song while *Naobi* could sing well but needed company. The other difference between the two teams was that *Nokma* and *Naobi* weren't sitting next to each other. Though I was a prodigy, I could clearly see *Naobi's* eyes were longing for *Nokma's* company. She would at times sing looking straight into the eyes of *Nokma* who couldn't see it as he was not sitting strategically and also that he was waiting for an opportunity to escape.

Naobi almost spoke her heart singing some fitting songs, but *Nokma* was poor in Hindi. Our team scored over in almost everything. We were discussing the songs in advance as that would bring the faces from either side in close proximity, and I was virtually being kissed in the process so many times.

We were served dinner on the very same table. The dinner was dry in the form of *puris and channa,* and the two girls joined me in the same plate. Ambience was such that on occasions, my mouth would receive a bite without my own hands being employed. The rains which had created havoc in the town were being celebrated in our dining hall that night.

Just when we finished the dinner, *Nokma* signaled his team to follow him, and shattered all the dreams which had a fair chance of being realized that night. Two girls won't allow me to go as they got hold of me. *Naobi* looked visibly upset, but *Nokma* was looking straight. I wish I could stop *Nokma* but he had already started walking.

"Don't go its risky. Ask him to stop." *Naobi* made an effort as she tried to persuade me.

I woke up to get outside the door where *Nokma* was already arranging for a jute string, which we were supposed to hold. All the three fellow men were ready leaving nothing much for me to do.

"Hey, *Nokma* I think we should stop here, it's risky."

"Come on, be fast, rain has stopped for a while, if there is an opportunity, this is the one, or else we won't be able to go." *Nokma* announced thus, diving into the water and throwing one end of the string towards me.

I had to follow reluctantly. I was more upset for the reason that I couldn't even had a last word with my fellow teammates before leaving. Also, I was upset for *Naobi* as she certainly had something to say that night.

"Who knows, the emotions are sometimes transitory and situational. *Nokma* lost this opportunity, for he couldn't realize the essence of timing in matters of love. He chose wild boar ahead of love." I jumped the streak, though disgusted and dejected.

The water was chest high, and we couldn't have reached had we not invented the technique of holding a jute rope, and taking our clothes off and tying them around our necks. The current tried to push us aside many a time but thankfully *Nokma* displayed tremendous experience, which he was clearly lacking while inside the dining hall. He clearly knew the trek and negotiated the current in a very professional manner. We just followed and reached the destination where water level had swollen well above our expectations.

EIGHT

FLOOD & FURY

The class room where we were supposed to lodge that night was a big hall, and the temporary platform we had erected by joining wooden benches was still intact though the water level had risen to an alarming level. The pause in rainfall was relieving and we decided to elevate the citadel further, to make it safe. The wooden benches were heavy and therefore unmoved by water. We climbed to the apex and that looked a safe destination prima facie.

Nokma immediately took to the dissection of his prized possession that night and tore it apart into the pieces of meat. To lit the fire was the most difficult job. Thankfully *Nokma* was carrying two pairs of match boxes. It took us an hour, only to lit the fire, and for that, one wooden bench which was not touched by water had to be sacrificed, thanks to the sharp daggers of *Nokma*. These wooden benches were procured by Principal somewhere from Bengal and were supposedly made up of *Sagwan* (Teak wood).

The pieces were pierced into by spokes of a bicycle wheel and were roasted on the flame produced by the teak wood, kept under a canister. This was one area where *Nokma* would not leave anything to chance. He had already arranged for some dry masala from the mess. Wild boar meat has an intense, sweet and nutty flavor due to its wild diet of grasses. It's slightly leaner and tends to be darker red than ordinary pork.

"Hey, what you guys ate in the dining hall. You all look hungry. You are eating like beasts." *Nokma* talked after very long time as he was too much into business till then.

"Why shouldn't we? After all we put in a lot of effort to meet the meat", answered one of our fellows.

"Yes really. We put in a lot of effort to meet the meat, and in the process even sacrificed the chance to mate", colloquially added another fellow of ours.

"Don't say like that, I never thought of her like that. It was just a plain feeling of love and nothing else." This intervention of *Nokma* relieved me to great extent as I thought the fellow comrade was taking a jibe on me, for he might have taken notice of my daredevils when I was sandwiched between the two pair of thighs.

"But *Nokma*, she wanted you to be there. She even asked me to stop you. I clearly saw love in her eyes. She sung for you the songs which meant confession of love." I narrated the whole story.

"What the hell? Why didn't you tell me earlier?" *Nokma* seemed annoyed.

"When did you listen but? I did try but you had jumped into water till then." I tried to explain.

"Oh my God, she must have been very upset. I think we must go to the dining hall now. It's risky here." *Nokma* suddenly turned the tables.

"Are you crazy *Nokma*? No we won't go, come what may." One of our fellows announced.

Nokma realized that none of us would turn up now. The rain had resumed and it was extremely difficult to cross those furious waters again.

Nokma however dared a single handed sojourn. He allowed us to sleep and escaped on a yet another adventure, though we took note of his leaving.

After about half an hour we again heard some sounds as *Nokma* was changing.

"What happened *Nokma*, Why you came back?"

"The water level has gone up and the current is impossible to negotiate. I was almost dragged by the water but thankfully survived." *Nokma* had a running nose and was sneezing badly. He went to sleep quickly.

We woke up to the sunlight when it sneaked in from the ventilator. The entire water had subsided leaving behind the mud and filth. The people in the mess were eager to see if we were alive. They felt happy when they saw us. The three girls were walking barefoot with their pants folded up to their knees and were taking stock of the situation. They looked at everything except us. They walked past us saying nothing, sparing not even a glance.

"You mustn't leave the burning fires alive, or you mustn't ignite them at all." *Nokma* kept his quite as the fellow comrade again took a jibe. May be *Nokma* had realized that the fellow comrade was right.

NINE
FAREWELL

The flood fury changed the dynamics of the campus completely. The wall around girl's hostel collapsed but that didn't help melting of the rift that had culminated in the dining hall the other day. Someone actually told the girls that we preferred a wild boar over the company of some beautiful girls or the hidden romantic appeals. The rain well just outside the dining hall, which served as meeting point for boys and girls on the pretext of washing plates, was washed away in floods. The girls won't have their meals in the dining hall; they would just pack it and leave for their hostel. The girls turned so indifferent that they even avoided our silhouettes. They would always remain in group and the decision to boycott us seemed unanimous.

The message was loud and clear, there was no chance left. We came back from daydreaming and it was time for studies. *Nokma* was yet to come out from the ordeal, but still was throwing him on the study table. Mishra sir would usually walk to hostel and counsel his students including *Nokma*. However, *Nokma* would routinely escape to his house and as a result his studies took a back seat.

Meanwhile the date sheet for final exams was announced. It was decided by the school authorities that the board classes would be given a farewell before exams. It was this day which brought *Naobi* and *Nokma* on the same table again, and here *Naobi* couldn't avoid *Nokma*.

"Hi *Naobi*, how are you?" *Nokma* broke the shackles.

"I am good. How are you?" *Naobi* managed only a half-smile.

"I am sorry for that day. I was told you sung for me. But you know my Hindi isn't that good, so I couldn't understand." Nokma tried to fill up the void.

"You don't even understand the emotions, the feelings; you understand nothing. You had killed a wild boar that day, right? You know how scared I was? I never saw floods in my life. I needed reassurances time and again, and my friends were on a hunt, risking their lives, Bravo." *Naobi* ventilated all her emotions revealing in the process that she desperately wanted to say all this, and was just looking for an opportunity.

Everyone was being called on stage to perform, to sing a song, or to have a few words. It was just when *Nokma's* name was announced.

"You know something, I have prepared a song for you, but I will sing only if you permit me." *Nokma* surprised *Naobi* by throwing ball in her court.

"What? Why are you asking me but?"

"Hurry up, all eyes are on us." *Nokma* pleaded.

"Okay, go and sing." *Naobi* completed in hurry.

Nokma woke up with a smile, climbed to the stage, addressed the gathering, and announced that he was going to sing a song. He took out a piece of paper and looked very confident. *Naobi* on the other hand was feeling goose bumps in her stomach.

"*Mere dil mein aaj kya hai, tu kahe to main bata dun*" (If you allow me, I can tell you what I hold in my heart for you), *Nokma* sung the same song which *Naobi* sang the other day in the dining hall, but was perhaps left incomplete as the wild boar had interrupted in between.

Nokma sang a little too badly and made a laughing stock of himself, but still went on to complete the song.

"Didn't I sing well? Why they all were laughing?" *Nokma* asked *Naobi* as he joined back after his performance.

"Stupid! Who asked you to sing?" *Naobi* burst into laughter.

As she recovered she noticed a teardrop in *Nokma's* eyes.

"Hey, you sung well. It doesn't matter to me." *Naobi* looked into his eyes holding his hand. *Nokma* was so broken that even *Naobi* holding his hand couldn't work.

"Hey *Nokma* please don't cry I will sing it for you again." *Naobi's* assurance helped *Nokma* back to his wits.

It was *Naobi's* turn to be on stage, and she chose to sing the same song.

"*Mere dil me aaj kya hai, tu kahe to main bata dun.*" She took everyone by surprise by almost announcing it publically.

Her voice was as sweet as a nightingale. *Nokma* was reciprocated in the most melodious manner. He understood every word of the song that day and fell for it. *Naobi* came back and again held his hand in assurance. They dinned together while occasionally looking into each other's eyes. There were many comments made by the onlookers' and passerby, but the couple responded in blushes only.

The story of the two blossomed as the exams neared. There were frequent meetings on the pretext of sharing notes. *Nokma* made his plans clear to *Naobi* that he wished to be a teacher after completing his Junior Basic training in teaching.

Naobi had always dreamt a very simple life for her. She wanted to start a music school with her younger sister and train small kids in classical music which they inherited from their grandma, who were a Bengali. Her mother was an exponent of Manipuri dance, and her father a government servant. They were a family of modern thoughts and she knew her parents wouldn't mind her marrying a person of her choice, provided, he was settled and preferably in Government job.

The proximity was not taken away with the commencement of exams even. They would see each other frequently and teachers came to know about their union. CBSC exams are month long process with huge breaks in between, and that gave them ample opportunities to grow more in love.

Finally the day came when we had to leave the place forever. *Naobi* was to leave for Manipur, and we for Himachal. *Nokma* was to be left all alone. All of us were crying perhaps for the reason that we would never get to see the place again, and that our paths may not cross again. Both *Nokma* and *Naobi* were assuring each other to stay in touch through letters and that they will surely meet again.

The bus station at *Baghmara* witnessed a massive turnout, gifts were exchanged, slam books were being written, addresses being exchanged, and on the sidelines tears being wiped out. The bus bound for *Tura* was the most warmly bidden adieu to. *Naobi* was in the same bus till we reached *Tura* and I could see her literally upset.

Two months later CBSC announced its results of class 12. *Nokma* didn't find his name in the list of students who had passed the exam. *Naobi* did manage to pass but her grades dropped drastically. The teenaged love affair had taken its toll.

Nokma couldn't believe this. He was devastated. There was no way one could enroll again in *Navodaya* Schools after having failed. Sense of guilt prevailed so much that *Nokma* sent someone else to collect his mark sheet. It was just then when *Naobi* stopped responding to *Nokma's* letters. *Nokma* was just two marks short in Hindi and three marks short in some other subject. The result changed the whole world for him. He had managed distinction in all the three other subjects, but that was rendered useless.

TEN

THE TROUBLED WATERS

Nokma desperately needed to earn. Their rice crop for the year was good but wasn't good enough to support the family financially. His mother was selling eggs from her poultry, but other than that there was no source of income. *Nokma's* presence in the house had increased the daily expanses manifold, as *Navodaya* Schools were absolutely free of cost schools, catering to everything ranging from boarding, lodging, dining, dresses, books and for that matter even the toothpaste, hair oil and shoe polish. Moreover, the school provided him an additional income from photography. He could have continued with photography in the campus itself since his house was near, but because of his result and the stigmatization associated with failures, the campus was automatically forbidden for him. Opening up of a studio seemed out of budget, as it would have required huge funds.

After thinking about for a month, *Nokma* reached a conclusion and decided to make money from fishing. He had done it with his father when he was a child but this time it was a different ball game altogether, as he wanted to do it commercially. He took a small loan from the nearby rural bank to buy a fishing net, and the locally crafted boat. He was sure that he needn't learn anything about fishing. He was a good sailor like most of the Garo men and therefore ventured into the business all alone.

Nokma started from river *Rompha*, which was comparatively a shallow one and with very small fish. He would throw his net in the middle and end up catching the stuff which wasn't edible, or at least saleable. Sometimes he would just get some small fish which he would throw back into the river. The whole day long exercise in the middle of river would hardly fetch him 50 rupees, but that wasn't going to be enough as going to Manipur someday was still in his mind.

"Aren't you trying to fish in loo? Go in for deep waters if you want big catches." An old lady ridiculed *Nokma's* effort the other day when he was counting his catches.

The whole night he kept on thinking catching something big the next day, and throw it back to the lady who ridiculed him. Come next morning and *Nokma* decided to sail to *Simsang* river.

The confluence of two rivers was at some good three kilometers distance from his house. Sun rises a bit too early in the northeastern parts of India giving a tough time for sailors. Both *Rompha* and *Simsang* are east flowing rivers so it obviously meant taking the scorching heat right on the face if you were sailing downstream. Even the sail downstream would take some real effort to reach a vast riverbed where most of the professional fishermen would flock.

Nokma noticed that none of them used advanced techniques of fishing and all were using traditional methods only. *Nokma's* presence raised some eyebrows but by and large it were only out of the inquisitive instinct, and not of the professional rivalry.

Fishing in river *Simsang* was bound to pay dividends as the river was home to many big and rare fishes. There were many small '*waris*' all along the river *Simsang*. *Wari* is a deep river pool where fish congregate when water levels are low. *Nokma* had discovered one such for him, and the *Chocolate Mahaseer, Shoals, Prawns* were some prominent catches his net would find. This extremely rich fish biodiversity has been a major source of livelihood for Garo people since ages, and *Nokma* joined the list of beneficiaries.

It resulted in 100/- rupees a day net profit for *Nokma*, plus a highly nutritious protein diet. His mother was also happy that he was right on the track. *Nokma* had never told his mother the outcome of his twelfth class result. On the contrary she was made to believe that he was pursuing his bachelors through correspondence.

Fishing was never easy however, as sometimes *Nokma* had even waited for three hours in a row, to find his first catch for the day. It took concentration of highest level to get one.

Sometimes he would wonder, "Had I put this much of concentration on my study table, it would have been a different story. I would have been doing the teacher's training and would still be receiving *Naobi's* letters. But what exactly did I want? Why I am thinking of different results. Eventually I would have been doing that for *Naobi*. Was she also a catch I was trying to woo, to get her entrapped in my net? Or was she clever enough to escape my net. Or was it me who had fallen prey to her?"

The sundry thoughts had many a time made *Nokma* drop a *Chocolate Mahaseer* as he would get a feeling that it was *Naobi* who got entrapped in his fishing net and he would sit quietly for hours hoping if it was *Naobi*, it would show up again. It would never happen though and *Nokma* would again resume his business.

After having fished for around three months, *Nokma* cleared his entire loan he had availed from the rural bank, but realized that this business was sufficient for livelihood but not good enough for a ticket to Manipur, where his love resided. This would make him restless.

He had been fishing for quite some time but he never talked to anyone sailing and fishing along. This was primarily because silence is almost a pre-condition for fishing.

After all it's a game of befooling your prey. They mustn't know about your presence or else they won't fall prey to your nets. This obviously resulted in automatic distancing amongst the fishermen in the river. The fishermen would settle for an imaginary territory and the jurisdiction thereof.

The other day when *Nokma* was docking his boat alongside the river bank, a man asked,

"How is your business going?"

"It's so-so, *Achhu*."

"You will pick up with time, no problem"

"What is the maximum one can earn from fishing?"

"On an average, not more than 150/- rupees a day. We don't have advanced boats, technology etc. There are some crooks who use dynamite, some will continue to fish in breeding season, some will use bleaching powder. There is no one to listen to the demands of fishermen. We have a society registered, but it's hopeless."

"*Achhu*, can't we enhance our daily wages if we go slightly deeper into the river. There must be a thick congregation there. I haven't seen anyone fishing there", *Nokma* asked.

Nokma made it that he was already earning 100/- rupees a day, and if he puts more efforts it can't go beyond 150/-. This will never make him rich; forget Manipur he can't even go beyond *Tura*.

"No you are not supposed to fish there, these are troubled waters." The old man cautioned.

"But, may I know why?" *Nokma* tried to be polite while asking a counter question.

"There are few conventions which need to be respected as they are. They are only for good." The old fisherman uttered his last words, as his mouth got preoccupied with areca nut, wrapped in fresh betel nut leaf and a dab of slaked lime.

Nokma however decided to take the stock of situation real time. It was lunch time for most of the fishermen and he took this opportunity for he just wanted to do a recce. He sailed to the point which looked near but was actually too far. He could feel the presence of a large fish congregation. He threw his net and it felt heavy within no time. He was surprised to see with the catch he had. He started putting all the fish in a large container on his boat. All of a sudden he faced a shock and couldn't remember what happened after that.

Nokma opened his eyes after a brief spell of time, almost blank to him. He found himself lying in his own boat docked aside. Some people were there keeping an eye on him.

"What happened to me? Where I am?" *Nokma* enquired.

"You went to fish in troubled waters and paid the price", replied the same old man who had advised him to not to venture into troubled waters.

"But what exactly happened? Will someone tell me?" *Nokma* still felt tremors in his body; his head was heavy and felt like he had a paralytic stroke.

"You were electrocuted by a fish you caught in your net. You must thank God that it was a mild attack. Otherwise it could have been your last fishing attempt." One another man explained.

"Electrocuted by a fish? What the hell are you talking about?"

"Yes there is a considerable presence of this fish called 'Electric ray', in the river *Simsang*. The fishermen are experienced enough to avoid the likely places where the fish dwells. It can give you a shock ranging up to 220 volts which can prove to be fatal. Our timely intervention saved you. Now you need to take rest for some days, and mustn't venture into that area again." The old man cautioned while everyone left to work seeing *Nokma* back into his senses.

Nokma was unconsciously taking out fishes from the net when he encountered one electric ray. It only acted in defense and discharged electric current to give electric shock to *Nokma*. He was noticed by a fellow fisherman who was heading for a lunch break and found *Nokma* en route, lying unconscious in his boat.

Nokma had all the troubles sailing back home, more so because the sail was upstream. He felt as if he was jolted from within. *Nokma* was still to decipher what this shock could have actually meant for him.

"Hope it wasn't *Naobi* this occasion. But it could be her. May be she doesn't want me to fish." The ideas thus cropped up in his mind.

It took nearly seven days for him to recover from the trauma but *Nokma* had decided to not to fish at all, leave aside in troubled waters. The shock spared his life but put it on a different track altogether.

ELEVEN
FARM FIASCO

Nokma had it approved from his mother that he will look after the fields from then on. The very first thing he needed to do was to buy a new pair of oxen. His mother used to hire them from neighbors but *Nokma* wanted his own as he was already contemplating commercial farming. There was one black color calf available in the vicinity and *Nokma* wasted no time buying it. It was however the search for its partner which went a little too long. Interestingly enough there was no calf available in the vicinity, of the same size *Nokma* having one.

The other day *Nokma* went to a nearby village in search of a calf. *Nokma* asked some people just outside the periphery of the village and he was told that there could be a possibility and they guided him towards a house.

The house looked beautiful, well decorated with flowers all around. There seemed a sizable presence of livestock. There was cattle shed at some distance as the smell of animal excreta confirmed it. A young looking girl just popped out of the window.

"Hi, Good morning, I am from the village nearby. I was actually looking for a calf to pair up with mine. Someone told me that there is a possibility here." *Nokma* wished the girl and revealed the purpose of his visit.

"Good morning, yes we do have one but we are also looking for a match. You can still have a look." The girl smiled and took *Nokma* to the cattle shed.

It was white calf of same size as that of *Nokma's*.

"Oh! This would be best match for my Julio." *Nokma* exclaimed in joy.

"Okay, then you can sell your Julio to us we and we can pair it with our Romeo." The girl laughed out loudly.

"But I am here to buy yours and not to sell my own", reiterated *Nokma*.

"I am afraid you won't be able to buy it. We have large paddy fields. We feed on them. How would we plough our fields if we don't have a pair of oxen?" The girl responded on a serious note.

Nokma stood there for a while, nodded his head in agreement and turned his back to move out.

"Hey, but the offer is still open the other way round. Why don't you sell your calf to us? It will make a good pair and we will pay you handsomely. My father is a good trainer and will make them work. Besides, you can also hire them alternately for your fields. Or you can plough our fields also and we can pay you for that." The girl threw an offer.

Nokma knew that he had no experience in training the calves to turn them into working oxen. Also, he knew that he doesn't have many options so he decided to agree to the proposal.

"Okay let me accept it for the sake of it, ma'am." *Nokma* said smilingly.

"I am *Daisy Sangma*, you can call me *Daisy*. What do I call you?"

"*Nokma*, everyone calls me like that, though I am not the one, the real *Nokma*."

They both smiled at this, and *Daisy* returned with a tea cup.

"You study?" *Nokma* asked while sipping from the cup.

"Not exactly, I failed in 12 class exams and now I don't feel like studying anymore. I am going to test my hand in farming, and will find someone like minded to get married." *Daisy* replied with no sense of regret. She looked confident with her future prospects.

"Oh I see, so who else is there in your house?" *Nokma* asked promptly.

"Only my father, he has gone to market. Both my elder brothers are married and they live in their own houses. I am the youngest of all." *Daisy* replied in one breath.

This typical eponymous tribal society is a matriarchal society. Girls marry their husbands to their own house, meaning thereby, the groom stays at bride's place unlike in other parts of the country. Since *Daisy* was youngest daughter she would essentially stay at her parent's house, making it obligatory for her husband to stay at her house.

Nokma wasn't thinking that far but still, "this is how it would go if at all it needed be", just a stray thought crossed *Nokma's* mind.

Things moved as per the expected lines. *Daisy's* father made a best combination by training the oxen into the skilled tillers. *Nokma* worked in tandem with *Daisy* and her father. *Daisy* had a knack for farming. She partly learnt it from her father and partly acquired through research and experience.

Daisy planned her project well and focused on land development first. She steered the land clear of stones and pebbles, freed it from all kinds of weeds, watered it suitably and then finally added the manures which she had made herself by mixing nitrogen rich leaves with excreta generated in her cattle shed.

They had a fair amount of land and she departed from the traditional over dependence on paddy, by introducing diversification of crops. She introduced vegetables and fruits in regular cropping patterns. The seasonal vegetables plus non seasonal one's using the concept of Greenhouses by regulating the temperature. She even continued the paddy cultivation in some parts using the seeds of some hybrid Basmati rice which increased their income manifold.

Nokma wasn't only tilling the fields but was learning very quickly. He adopted the same technique in his own fields. He would wake up at four in the morning and would work in his fields till six. His mother would take care of fields afterwards. At seven he would sail his boat down to *Daisy's* house which was at one kilometer's distance away, en route to *Baghmara* market. He will have the *Daisy's* special breakfast and would take all the vegetable plucked and packed by her father, to *Baghmara* market. His fishing boat was also employed in the process. After selling the vegetable he would sail back to have lunch with Daisy and her father. They would work in the fields till evening and then *Nokma* would head back to his house to have dinner with his mother.

Nokma's income also grossed manifold. He used the same market for his own products as well. Daisy's farms were already doing rounds and she was selling them for prices at will. *Nokma* besides getting paid handsomely by *Daisy*, was also earning from his own fields. His mother was working very hard and *Nokma* was providing the technical expertise besides managing some time for his own fields routinely.

This was quite a busy routine and they all were so much into the business that they didn't even realize that it were already three years since they have been working together. *Daisy* was a true professional and she minded only her work. She also shared her knowledge with other farmers. It wasn't only *Nokma* who was benefitting from her expertise but there were several others. *Daisy* had already made the headlines and as a result was invited to *Shillong* to be felicitated as one of the progressive farmers.

It was at *Shillong* where she met the man of her dreams. *Wiking Marak* had done his masters in agriculture and wanted to opt for farming as a full time job. *Wiking Marak* was a thorough gentleman and *Daisy* straightway proposed him for marriage. It turned out to be an alliance of convenience as *Wiking Marak* had dreams but not the land at suitable place. *Daisy* unfolded everything in front of him and they happily agreed to tread together.

Nokma never really felt anything for *Daisy* but still the news of her getting married didn't go smoothly down his throat. Though he took part in the widely celebrated marriage and looked involved. There was grand celebration as a huge party was thrown after all the rituals at the church.

After the celebrations were over it was the business as usual for *Daisy*. *Wiking* also joined the fields with his expertise and as a result the working hours for *Nokma* increased slightly. *Wiking* didn't like *Nokma's* working in own fields and would want him to work full time with them. *Nokma* realized it but he knew that still *Daisy* wanted him to work with them. Their association also irked *Wiking* but he didn't have the authority to expel *Nokma* or the valid reasons to press for it.

So he started looking for opportunities.

The other day when *Nokma* was taking a nap after ploughing the field, *Wiking* deliberately untied the oxen and they went berserk in the vegetable field. This irritated *Daisy* badly.

"How can you be so irresponsible? Do you even have an idea how much we have lost?"

In the meantime *Wiking Marak* stepped in ferociously.

"I don't think it's a good idea to continue with him. You better pack up man!"

"No, let us give him a chance. This is only the first time he committed a mistake." *Daisy* came to *Nokma's* rescue.

"Come on *Daisy*, he doesn't deserve. We can manage without him." *Wiking Marak* insisted.

Nokma stood quite for some time. He was taken aback by all this. He felt insulted.

"Thank you so much for everything. You don't have to advocate any more for me *Daisy*. I always thought myself to be a partner in this venture, but I was wrong. I was only a servant." *Nokma* was dejected and had tears in his eyes. He left immediately without even asking for the remunerations.

TWELVE

SAIL TO STRIFE

The incident jolted *Nokma* from within. He felt insulted and confined himself in his house for many days. He couldn't even work in his own fields.

It was an off season for paddy crop, and since he didn't have greenhouses, vegetables and fruits were out of question. *Nokma* was bored and this propelled him for small outings to local market. He would have tea and would watch people playing cards. They would sometimes play for cash and gamble. *Nokma* would enjoy watching them.

One fine evening *Nokma* noticed two strangely new faces having a game of rummy, while managing both playing cards and cigarettes in their hands, in a small tea shop. They were also having booze, locally made of rice. The men were in their forties, wearing jeans and T-Shirts, and had their sunglasses placed on the table. There was also a helmet, as the men had travelled in Yamaha RX-100 motor cycle. They looked professional gamblers and won't talk much.

Nokma started watching the game with utmost interest. The two men finished a full aluminum container of wine and finished their rivals almost effortlessly. They collected all the money and ordered tea for everyone standing out there. As the tea vendor called upon *Nokma* to fetch his glass, the men overheard this.

"Is he the *Nokma*?" asked one of the men.

"No, my father was. He died in an accident. People started calling me like that." *Nokma* interrupted before anyone else could.

"The same accident which took place at borders in the river *Simsang*, right?" asked the other men to notice many others nodding in agreement, though *Nokma* remained silent on this.

"Come on have a seat." The other men moved further on a wooden bench to accommodate *Nokma*.

Nokma reluctantly occupied the seat.

"What you do?"

"Nothing much. Don't have a work."

"How about working with us?"

"What's the work?"

"Will explain only if you are interested. We can pay you 10000/- rupees for just one day."

Nokma was open mouthed on listening 10000/- for one day. He hadn't been paid for last many days.

"Yes I would work, no matter what it is."

"Okay you can come tomorrow, the same place and we will let you know the work." The men advanced 5000/- rupees in advance to *Nokma*.

Nokma didn't want to receive the money but the man put it forcibly in his hands. They quickly moved out, kick started the bike and disappeared in no time.

Nokma convinced himself that if he didn't like the work he would return the advance and that he won't take tensions before even knowing the nature of work.

Next evening the men arrived a bit too late and there weren't too many people left at the tea shop. As soon as they arrived they ordered tea and made *Nokma* to sit on a corner table.

"So what exactly have I been paid for?" *Nokma* asked.

"Ah! We will just give you a bag, which you will have to take across the borders, stealthily swimming under the waters of *Simsang* river. Our man will collect it from you on the other side and will help you get back via land route."

"What? Are you crazy? I won't do it." *Nokma* put the entire money on table.

"That isn't the option available with you now. You have already accepted the advance, be very sure about it. You can deny only the next deliveries; for this you have been paid. It would amount to loss of lakhs to the market and you may end up facing repercussions of severest measures." One of the men alarmed in a husky voice.

"May I know what is there in this packet?" *Nokma* asked with a shivering voice.

"There are tiger bones in it. They will further be transported to Burma where they are used in the manufacturing of certain drugs." The other man revealed the mystery.

"What if I am caught?" *Nokma* dared to ask again in a shaky voice.

"We don't know you then. You will get your remaining money only if you come back safe." The men announced in unison.

"How do I do it but?" *Nokma* appeared slightly more confident in this ask.

"You will start early in the morning on a boat and would dock it just before the border area. You can see the tower alongside, with some guards on it and lights flashing. Here you have to immerse yourself underwater and swim across around 500 meters like a submarine. After the relaxed swimming for around 1.5 kilo meters, you again need to go underwater for about 500 meters to evade the eye of BDR (Bangladesh rifles) jawans. There you will see lot of boats docked alongside and you will get into boat with number 70 inscribed on it in bolds. Rest of the things will be explained to you there and then." The man unfolded the details.

"Now we have to move as we are already late. It's for your safety that you shouldn't be seen with us by many." The men put the bag wrapped in polythene alongside the stash of five thousand rupees and left the shop, leaving *Nokma* in the lurch.

Nokma couldn't sleep the whole night. "May be this is how my father was entrapped. May be they are the people responsible." So many ideas kept coming to his mind before he could sleep in wee hours.

Nokma woke up early and started sailing down to the point where he needed to reach before taking the swimming route. He docked his boat, wore the bag around his back and started swimming. It turned extremely easy with downstream. He spotted the BSF tower and immersed himself under the water. After clearing the distance he pulled his head out to take a breath. It was morning and his fitness was helping him a great deal. After swimming a good distance he spotted the BDR tower and he again torpedoed himself to a fair distance. The job was done but he felt a severe kind of jolt in his left leg while he was swimming under the water. He thought maybe it was electric fish which gave him the jolt. He continued swimming till he found the boat without moving his leg much.

The boat man readily recognized him and signaled him in. *Nokma* advanced the packet and lied tiredly on the boat. The boatman speeded in no time. After a while the boatman noticed blood coming out from *Nokma's* leg.

"Where the hell is that coming from?" Boatman spoke chaste Bengali.

"Maybe I encountered an electric fish." *Nokma* thankfully could speak and understand Bengali.

He sailed sidereal and docked it on reaching the bank to have a look what went wrong.

"Oh my God! This is a bullet injury. You have been hit. I can't take you with me now, or else we will all be in trouble. You are bleeding and with this packet with us, which I need to drop at its destination in stipulated time, it doesn't sound wise. You need medical care but we can't take you to hospital as it will be a police case. You alight here on river bank and I will come back with some first aid and medicines." The boatman announced.

The men patrolling the borders on either side would sometimes fire few rounds into the river blindly, and sometimes even across the border to keep the trespassers guessing. It's very difficult to border the flowing waters, and hence even the cross border firings were not opposed to as long as the target remained water. *Nokma* was hit by one unfortunate wild shot and the nationality of the gun barrel which fired the shot remained a mystry.

Nokma didn't feel the pain initially as his body was warmed up to a great degree, and the morning cold water must also have helped. But he started feeling it slowly as his body started cooling and he started losing his sense of reasoning slowly.

The boatman had raced away in no time. *Nokma* got off the boat and lied down, beneath a tree

Nokma had a look at his wound. The bullet had just edged passed his leg but a pallet got stuck on the edge of his leg calf. He immediately scraped it out with the help of a pointed bamboo split.

In excruciating pain he cleansed his wound thoroughly with a piece of cloth torn from his cotton shirt to rule out the possibility of leaving even a trace of pallet, and dressed it tightly with his cotton shirt. The blood stopped but the pain was unrelenting. He had some water, dragged himself slightly deep into the jungle and lied down under a tree to wait for boatman and for the first aid, or maybe the second aid as he already had the first.

THIRTEEN

THE RESURRECTION

Nokma lied half conscious and went to sleep in bits and pieces, though he could always feel the pain. He could only open his eyes to see around and confirm if he was safe. It was only the next morning he discovered that the boatman hadn't come and perhaps was never going to come. There were two issues which needed immediate addressal. The first one to bother was the hunger as he was quite accustomed to the pain by then. *Nokma* tried to wake up but could only with the help of holding the branches of small shrubs around. He tried to walk but that was not possible as the leg ached more while moving. Still he dragged himself to the river bank, without bending the leg which hurt. He reached a place where huge debris of waste fish lied, which possibly would have resulted from the process of grading and packing them for further sale in the market. Most of them were small fish rendered useless for sale by fishermen and were smelling bad. *Nokma* found some relatively fresher ones and yet to be decayed fish. There was one other waste debris lying nearby, from where *Nokma* collected a water can, an iron rod and a match box.

Nokma went back to the place where he had spent his previous night. There was a small stream oozing out of the laterite soil and eventually mixing into the giant river. At the mouth of it, water was quite clean and drinkable. *Nokma* filled his water can. He lit fire and baked the fish. *Nokma* could eat even the uncooked fish but they were not fresh and he knew it could be dangerous. After this small feast *Nokma* felt energized and his sense of reasoning restored to a fair degree.

The second most important thing was to take care of his wound. He carefully rolled out the dressing from deep inside the skin; it had used the blood as an adhesive to stick firmly around his leg. The exercise turned out to be extremely painful but it had to be done in any case. He again cleansed it with a wet cotton cloth and placed his leg before the fire so as to dry it. The pain resumed manifold and that's when the *Sylvester Stallone* of *Rambo*, taking care of his wound surfaced in his mind. The movies of *Rambo* series were most watched movies during school days. He heated a metal rod to dull red, and brought the wound in contact with it for good two to three seconds. He literally screamed out of pain to disturb the morning calm of the place. He again wrapped the clean dry cotton cloth around the wound and extinguished the fire. He didn't want the smoke to reveal his presence in the thick jungle around. Excruciating pain didn't allow him to sleep but still he kept lying under the tree. The atmosphere was hot and humid so body was detoxifying faster. *Nokma* kept on drinking water to avoid dehydration without even feeling the urge to unleash loo.

Nokma woke up in the afternoon to discover that the pain was reduced to a considerable extent. The thermal shock must have burnt the outer cells dead or destroyed some tissues, and that's what could have been the reason for respite from pain. He could walk with reduced effort so he decided to establish a rapport with the surroundings.

Simsang or *Someshwari* in Bangladesh has a vast biodiversity on either bank. The banks are invariably covered with riparian forests. As he moved slightly deep into the forest he could find Chameleon plant (*Macha Duribak*), a medicinal plant widely used for blood purification. There were *Gaultheria* leaves which are used for body ache, and above all the *Gotu Kola*. In Meghalaya *Gotu Kola* herb is known as all in one medicine, widely used by indigenous healers to treat all kinds of ailments. *Gotu Kula* is a time tested remedy with amazing health benefits. *Nokma's* mother had always used these plants as medicine and therefore *Nokma* had a fair idea about the usage. He picked up everything in proportion for at least ten days and came back.

Nokma knew that this was the wettest place and he was only lucky that I didn't rain so far. He knew how to make a house for him under these circumstances but didn't have the equipment. At least a billhook was required. He just searched some bamboo sticks and made a boundary wall for him under the thick leaves of a lowly branch of a *Saal* tree. It was just at a suitable height to serve the roof, which would hardly allow rains to filter in. The Garo houses are mostly woven from thin bamboo threads and *Nokma* had mastered the technique while his house was being constructed. He covered a place of his size from all the four sides with bamboo woven walls by crisscrossing the bamboo splits into one another. Within three hour of perspiration *Nokma* was in a house which was roofed, had a boundary wall to save him from the wild animals, and had a slightly elevated floor with some wooden planks and with soft dry grass distributed on them.

Nokma also realized that his body was in dire need of proteins to repair his cells and for that there was no option better than the fish. The debris near the river bank was good option but he had to score over the birds hovering around, who were also the legitimate beneficiaries of the feast. Small fish rendered useless were always a possibility, and *Nokma* relied on this option only. However, he ventured with utmost care so that no one could take notice of him, or at least establish his identity.

Nokma decided to lodge himself there temporarily while monitoring carefully his wound. He avoided the daily dressings but made sure it didn't get wet. He simultaneously kept taking regular doses from the collections of his medicinal plants. He was only feeling improvement day after day.

The other day he climbed to a decent height to have a view around. The river was vast but still height gave him a fair idea about the directions and coordinates. He was sure that he would be returning via land route only, as swimming upstream was a virtual impossibility. The boatman who was supposed to tell him the tricks of getting back, never really got back. Therefore *Nokma* decided to decode the route. The bazar nearby was a good three kilometers sail downstream, *Nokma* gathered from gleaming lights. There was also an abandoned boat near the debris, *Nokma* had already gathered. "Ascertaining anything more from this place could be disastrous", *Nokma* concluded. However, he was in no hurry. He was a hunter, and hunting had taught him one thing, the patience. Not only you can lose your prey, but at times can fall prey for want of patience.

After ten days, *Nokma* woke up early in the dark hours one morning and tested him for fitness. He ran on the sands of river, he also tried his strength in swimming. Though he could do this but with reduced capacity. He also checked the boat by actually taking it into the waters. Boat was in good shape and was working. *Nokma* threw an abandoned fishing net into spiraling waters of *Someshwari*, which returned with a couple of fresh fish.

Nokma came back before the break of dawn to escape the eyes of fishermen, who were yet to arrive. He put everything back in place, headed to his transient camp, had his fresh breakfast and retired. He wanted to monitor his leg's response after that small session. After the whole day's observation, it was all good. No pain was felt and everything looked good.

FOURTEEN

IN ALIEN LAND

Next morning *Nokma* woke up a little too early to start the sail to a destination which was unknown to him. He tried his luck by throwing the abandoned fishing net lying in the boat in the river, and was prized with two big fish adding up to five kilos to his boat. The sail was easy downstream, and *Nokma* reached in no time. He alighted on the bank which was a gateway to an unknown town and allowed the boat to sail down, may be to Bay of Bengal.

The town was yet to wake up to the morning. There were few fishermen helping their boats to let lose in the waters of river *Someshwari*. There was no signboard written in English, and hence *Nokma* couldn't find the name of the town. *Nokma* could speak Bengali, but couldn't read. The dark subsided in no time to allow the morning light to take control of the small town. *Nokma* was walking with fish in his hands. He saw an old lady fanning the coal oven in her small tea shop. *Nokma* spontaneously longed for tea seeing this.

"You need *Mahaseer Thakuma*? They are fresh, just got them."

"Don't fish that too early. *Koi takka*?" (For how many?).

"Whatever you think is right?"

"*Panch Takka. Cha khabe na ki?*" Grandma offered five *Takka* and a cup of tea.

Nokma agreed readily. Tea tasted best, so much so that he asked the lady to give him one more cup.

"*Thakuma*, when they open the gates at border to allow people to crossover?" *Nokma* played a blind shot.

"You got to queue up early. They are very strict now, they ask your name and village and count when back in the evening. Smuggling has increased manifold in the recent past." Grandma (Thakuma) told.

Nokma thanked grandma, put five *Takka* in his pocket, and started moving fast. He located the road and started treading along the river *Someshwari* in the opposite direction. Those who sail have better sense of direction, and *Nokma* was sailing for quite some time. He believed his gut feeling and continued moving.

Nokma wasn't wearing anything above his waist as his shirt was already lost to the repeated dressings of his wound. He was wearing only a pant folded up to the point, which was well below the point where he was hit. Though Garo men don't generally grow whiskers, but some bushy pines had emerged from *Nokma's* face. His face and skin had tanned badly, but to give him an advantage; he resembled the people who were in the fray to cross the borders for their daily earnings.

The daily wages were astoundingly higher just three kilometers away on the other side of the border, and that propelled some to work there for the entire day and come back in the evening. The officials on the both sides were liberal to these poor people but there have been untoward incidents many a times. Some of them would stay put and slowly sneak deep into the territory creating demographic imbalances, normally referred to as *Chakma* refugees. Also there were stray incidents of smuggling the petty small things to avoid the custom and import duties. However, the biggest threat was the narcotics, which were smuggled to Myanmar via Bangladesh, and that was responsible for the strictness imposed at the borders.

Nokma joined the queue without looking worried. He was gifted with utmost calmness and composure. His only problem was that he didn't know where he was coming from.

"Where are you from?" *Nokma* whispered in ears of a man standing next to him.

"*Baghmara*, no sorry, I am from *Durgapur*." The man fumbled with words and *Nokma* understood in no time that they were the chips of same block.

There was a *jawan* standing and frisking everyone, and then he would allow them one by one for a little interview with a man who was sitting on a wooden chair and looked someone higher in the rank.

The man frisking didn't allow *Nokma* to travel with 5 *Takkas*. He confiscated the currency and asked him to collect when he would be back in the evening. Nokma realized that two tea cups had cost him five *Takkas*, but gave them happily as he knew they weren't of any value to him beyond that point. *Nokma* advanced further after clearing the man.

"Write down your name and address on the register." The official asked.

"I can't read and write." *Nokma* refused politely.

"I want your name, your village, and whether have you gone earlier?"

"I am *Partho* from *Durgapur*, going for the first time."

"Remember one has to come back. I will destroy your family and house in Durgapur if you have something else in your mind." The official gave him some fierce looks before he signalled the next one.

Nokma passed but noticed that the man, who confused *Baghmara* and *Durgapur* and was standing next to him, was detained and asked to wait in a small kiosk for further enquiry. He must have fumbled again *Nokma* gathered.

After clearing the BDR check post *Nokma* had to travel some 500 meters the land, which was probably no man's land. Surprisingly a small piece of land having extremely tight security on either side was lying unattended.

Then came the BSF check post, where a *Sardarji* was looking after the routines. *Sardarji* was taking no notes but was watching his subjects with penetrating eyes.

"*Udhar kab gaya tha?*" (When did you cross?). *Sardarji* asked with a ferocious voice.

Nokma stood puzzled as if he didn't understand what *Sardarji* had said.

This worked for *Nokma* and he allowed him to go. *Nokma* made out that even if the person detained by BDR was allowed, he would fall for the grilling of *Sardarji*. *Sardarji* would use this technique and had held many. It was only the poise of *Nokma* which helped him.

Most of the persons were engaged in coal mining and timber cutting. However, they were allowed the access to local market to buy some essentials. *Nokma* took the other route and escaped to *Baghmara* market where he had lunch in a small eatery managed by his friend.

He rode pillion the bicycle of his neighbor from the village and reached home. He was tired so ruled out the river route and sailing his boat back. His mother was a bit worried but her fears were brushed aside by some instantly concocted stories woven by *Nokma*.

FIFTEEN

THE FOLLOW UP

After having reached home, *Nokma* rested to sleep for two consecutive days. He was so tired that all efforts of his mother to wake him up went in vain. He woke up after two days to take bath, to shave off his bushy whiskers, to have his meals and then finally to have a look at his wound. It looked healed but he felt a kind of strain or tension while walking, so he thought of taking a medical opinion. He left for Guwahati to see a specialist surgeon, citing a minor blast at fishing sight the reason for his wound. Doctor took several X-rays to establish that some part of the skin was still infected and that it needed to be removed surgically. *Nokma* was consequently operated upon and was advised two weeks rest before a follow up, and during this period he was to remain in the hospital under medical supervision.

The other day when *Nokma* was resting, an unknown man visited him and advanced a bundle five thousand rupees to him.

"Sorry, I didn't recognize you, and why this money?"

"This is the remaining money which was promised to you after the completion of assignment. You are however directed to be as confidential as you have been till now and not to disclose anything, come what may." The man put the money in the cupboard adjacent to the bed *Nokma* was lying, and fled immediately.

Nokma remained puzzled for the moment, but decided to count his share after some time. To his surprise the notorious gang had remained faithful with him.

After two weeks *Nokma* was discharged but with host of medicines, though he felt better. He again rested for two weeks back home till he was completely fit. *Nokma* had enough money from the assignments he took up in the recent past but still he felt the need to work. He didn't want to sail again while he had already ruled out the possibility of fishing also. Agriculture and farming became out of question. The one that fetched him ten thousand rupees was the last thing in his mind. He was desperate to try and work something different, but didn't know what to do?

One fine day while he was having tea in the nearby village tea stall, he heard a conversation among sitters that a photography competition was being held at *Baghmara*, and that the best one would compete at North Eastern States Photography competition to be held in *Manipur* the next month. This excited *Nokma* as he immediately asked for the details.

The competition was actually a qualifying round for North Eastern States Photography competition, and the participants could enter with as many entries. The theme of the competition was essentially the harmony between men and nature.

Nokma scanned all his photographs reaching home. A lot many of them were damaged due to moisture, but still those in album were spared by fungus. Keeping in view the theme and after so many shuffles, *Nokma* finally selected a photograph and convinced himself that his would be a single entry only. The photograph which had *Naobi* holding a pitcher plant, the one he clicked near his house. Pitcher plants are actually carnivorous and may have negative connotations, but *Nokma* still decided to move on with the picture due to *Naobi's* presence. *Nokma* searched for its negative and got it enlarged. He himself framed it beautifully with the help of a local carpenter.

On the appointed day, *Nokma* dressed himself to best of his dressing sense, took blessings of his mother, went to the church, and finally submitted his entry completing all the codal formalities once he reached the *Baghmara* Police ground. There were host of other photographers not just representing *Garo* hills but also from *Khasi* Hills and *Jaintia* Hills. *Nokma* had a look on the photographs which were exhibited on the walls of a makeshift room. All the pictures were stunningly clicked and were theme based. The winner was to be adjudged by a three membered jury, comprising the principal of *Navodaya* School also.

It was *Nokma's* photograph which sieged the day. Pitcher plant being the rarest, the state was running several pilot projects to conserve and multiply its numbers. One such project was there in *Baghmara* itself.

"The photograph depicted the cultivation and conservation of a rare plant in the kitchen garden, and the tender hands holding it with a rare smile, a classic case of human harmony with nature." Thus wrote the Principal who had taken away *Nokma's* employment three years back by putting off the contract of clicking passport size photographs.

The jury seemed agreed with Principal and *Nokma* won a new Canon camera, besides a ticket to *Bishnupur* town of *Manipur* for final round of North Eastern States Photography competition.

SIXTEEN

TOO CLOSE BUT TOO FAR

Nokma embarked on a journey which he had waited for long. There was a catch in this photography competition; it was an opportunity to see *Naobi*. He knew that *Naobi* hailed from *Bishnupur* itself. He didn't forget to carry the address with him, though he had stopped writing letters to her but address was always there, safely written on his diary.

Nokma alighted in the beautiful town which wasn't very far from *Imphal*. The ancient town of *Bisnupur* is immaculately beautiful and it instantly caught the eye of *Nokma*. The staying arrangements for all the participants were made in a small but beautiful tourist lodge near *Loukoipat* Lake. After retiring and refreshing, all the participants exchanged pleasantries and decided to have a feel of town. Most of them decided to visit the ancient Vishnu temple, but *Nokma* decided otherwise.

Nokma escaped to the address he had written many letters to. It was a small house and *Nokma* entered without any hesitation. He was greeted by a young girl, who must have been *Naobi's* younger sister.

"Hello, I was actually looking for *Naobi*. I have come here for the North Eastern States Photography competition, all the way from Meghalaya. We were actually class mates in *Navodaya* School." *Nokma* smiled while revealing the details.

"Are you *Nokma*?" The young girl exclaimed.

"Oh yes, how do you know that?" *Nokma* responded with double joy.

"Come on in." She opened the door for *Nokma*.

Nokma seated on a wooden chair and sensed there was none other present in the house.

As she came out with a glass of water *Nokma* readily asked, "Is *Naobi* out for some work?"

"Ah! Actually I am very sorry to tell you that *Naobi* is no more."

"What? What happened, and how?" *Nokma* put the glass back on table.

"There were frequent clashes between *Naga* and *Kuki* during those days when she came back from Meghalaya. She was collecting donations for her dream music school while continuing her studies through correspondence. One unfortunate evening she was caught in crossfire that injured her badly. She remained in hospital for about a month but succumbed to injuries eventually. She kept on talking about you, and told me that one day you will definitely come looking for her. She wrote answers to your letters even but never posted them." The girl started sobbing.

Nokma kind of felt shot again, but bang on the heart this occasion. He lost all his excitement. He didn't know what to say.

"Her sacrifice didn't go in vain though. They announced ceasefire the very next day to regret her death. She was awarded posthumously by the government. We in turn are running a music school in her memory." *Naobi's* sister realized that *Nokma* was shocked deeply so she tried to heal by something positive.

Nokma didn't say anything. He was devastated. He carefully examined the date of her passing away written on a photograph placed on a cupboard, it was the same day he was shocked by an electric fish. He got up quickly and left. The girl couldn't find an appropriate response; she didn't even ask him to stay back.

The very next morning it was all set for the mega event. Chief Minister was to preside over the function. *Nokma* didn't sleep the whole night and wanted to leave soon once the function was over.

Naobi was immensely recognized and respected by one and all. She was easily identifiable in that photograph of *Nokma*, and jury had no problems whatsoever to adjudge *Nokma's* photograph the best. Chief Minister himself spoke to *Nokma* while handing over a cash prize of Ten thousand rupees. *Nokma* literally cried on stage.

Nokma came back to the tourist lodge and didn't celebrate his victory. All his fellow competitors from all the states of North East congratulated him and offered him the party but *Nokma* refused. They were scheduled to leave the next morning, but before that *Nokma* decided to visit *Naobi* memorial music school.

The school was being run in a yet to be completed building. *Naobi's* sister was the principal in charge. She came out as she saw *Nokma*.

"Hi, I am sorry I left all of a sudden from your house the other day. I need a favor from you. Please except this money as a grant for the school." *Nokma* handed over the entire prize money of ten thousand rupees to the young girl.

"Come on let me show you something." She pulled *Nokma's* hand and dragged him in after taking the money.

The photograph which was adjudged best in the competition, was hanging on the wall of conference hall of the school. *Naobi's* smile holding that pitcher plant in *Nokma's* courtyard had made the hall so vibrant that *Naobi* could actually be felt there.

"The organizers gifted this painting to the *Naobi* memorial school while simultaneously agreeing to sanction a grant in aid of Ten thousand rupees. That Photograph of yours has once again reminded people about the sacrifice of *Naobi*. Otherwise she was on the verge of being forgotten." She seemed lost for a moment.

"You know something; I have a special gift for you." She handed over the letters written by *Naobi* in response to *Nokma's* letters.

"Wish you all the best. I would want the children to sing as good as *Naobi* sung. Write me whenever there is a need of any kind." *Nokma* wished young girl and left after clicking some pictures of the campus and of the children along with their Principal in his new Canon camera.

He boarded the bus to start the journey back to his place. He took out one of the letters and started reading it as the bus started moving out of the town negotiating the curvy labyrinths. With every word *Nokma* literally felt her. *Naobi* seemed to be reading it out herself. There were tears in his eyes as he read a paragraph from the letter.

"I am working very hard for the donations to start my school. I expect some money from you as well. But don't worry, not now, but when you will start earning and visit my place. You know something? Other day I dreamt as if you have won an award for your best photo and you came to my school to donate your entire prize money."

Nokma folded the letter to put it back in the envelope. He couldn't read even a single word after that. His eyes dried all of a sudden. He opened the window to swing his head out of it. He felt drizzles on his face and the gushes of cold breeze unfurled his hair. It didn't feel like a return journey, but rather a new journey to some unknown destination, as the bus moved past the small, evergreen hills.

9 7 9 8 8 8 6 6 7 4 6 7 5